Raffy the first Giraffe

Order this book online at www.trafford.com/07-1935
or email orders@trafford.com

Most Trafford titles are also available at major online book retailers.

Note for Librarians: A cataloguing record for this book is available from Library
and Archives Canada at www.collectionscanada.ca/amicus/index-e.html

Printed in Victoria, BC, Canada.

ISBN: 978-1-4251-4552-1

*We at Trafford believe that it is the responsibility of us all, as both individuals and corporations,
to make choices that are environmentally and socially sound. You, in turn, are supporting this
responsible conduct each time you purchase a Trafford book, or make use of our publishing services.
To find out how you are helping, please visit www.trafford.com/responsiblepublishing.html*

*Our mission is to efficiently provide the world's finest, most comprehensive book publishing
service, enabling every author to experience success. To find out how to publish your book, your
way, and have it available worldwide, visit us online at www.trafford.com/10510*

TRAFFORD PUBLISHING   www.trafford.com

North America & international
toll-free: 1 888 232 4444 (USA & Canada)
phone: 250 383 6864 ♦ fax: 250 383 6804 ♦ email: info@trafford.com

The United Kingdom & Europe
phone: +44 (0)1865 722 113 ♦ local rate: 0845 230 9601
facsimile: +44 (0)1865 722 868 ♦ email: info.uk@trafford.com

10 9 8 7 6 5 4 3 2

About the Author

Malcolm G. Aikman

The Illustrator

Jesus S. Salvacion

Malcolm retired from the accounting profession several years ago and developed an interest in writing stories for children. He has written several short stories to help children understand concepts such as evolution, animal behavior and characteristics. Raffy is the first of these stories to be published. He intends to assist his early readers to enjoy reading and develop a love for books. His stories are filled with adventure and lovable characters that mirror the beauty of nature that surrounds us.

Jess' illustrations and animations aim to portray the freshness of a story with simplicity and its use of vibrant colors. A nurse by profession , he injects in his drawings an enthusiasm for life. Having two children of his own he knows the importance of maintaining the purity of a child's innocence. This desire is evident in all of his artwork.

Raffy was a sort of antelope, a fairly ordinary looking one, with a brown and white dappled coat and two short horns on top of his head. He had one special talent. Raffy was insatiably curious. He needed to know everything that went on in Karanga, where he lived.

One day Raffy came upon a fence. It hadn't been there the last time he passed this way so he decided to find out what was on the other side.

He followed the fence looking for a way through. He found a gate, but it was closed and Raffy couldn't see beyond it. He tried to look over the fence but it was just a little too high.

Raffy was really annoyed because he desperately wanted to know what was happening on the other side. All day long he strained with his legs and neck but still couldn't see over the top. "I'll come back tomorrow and try again" he thought.

4

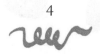

The next day Raffy arrived at the fence. All day he strained with all his might. By bedtime he felt his neck had stretched just a little bit and he could almost see over the top. "Tomorrow I should be able to do it", he vowed as he trotted off home.

Meanwhile old Mr. Pontifract, who had built the fence to protect his flower garden from hungry antelopes like Raffy, had noticed the two horns peeking over the top. "I'll fix that antelope" he said to his wife that evening and went out to add two more inches to his fence.

The following morning Raffy arrived just after breakfast. Again he tried to look over the top, but didn't realize that two inches had been added. He strained and strained. Once more he felt his neck stretch just a little bit. Maybe even his legs stretched too, since his eyebrows just reached to the top of the fence. He was closer but still couldn't quite see over.

Mr. Pontifract had been watching from his garden and saw the horns and eyebrows as they appeared over his fence. So out he went that evening and added another two inches.

This went on for a whole week.
Each day Raffy strained and stretched.

Each day Mr. Pontifract added two more inches to the top of his fence.

Meanwhile Raffy's family was grazing as usual. A whole week had gone
by before his father turned to say something to him and was surprised
to find he had to tilt his head up to look Raffy in the eye. 'My word'
exclaimed Raffy's father. 'I used to look down at you.'

Raffy continued to go to the fence each day, trying to see over the top.

Each day Mr. Pontifract added more fencing
and it grew
and grew
and grew.

So did Raffy. Well actually it was his neck and front legs that grew most as he stretched and stretched.

One day, as he was trying to add still another two inches to his fence, Mr. Pontifract felt a pain in his chest.

His wife took him off to the doctor who told him he had stop working and rest. By this time the fence was 15 feet high.

Raffy arrived the following day and strained and strained and strained. Suddenly, to his great delight and astonishment, he peeked over the top of the fence and saw the garden. "Oh, it's just another garden. Isn't that the pits!'

Feeling annoyed and disappointed, he lost interest.

But as Raffy turned away he realized for the first time how far his head was from the ground.

Then he noticed that he had to spread his legs apart to reach down to the stream and drink water. 'That's strange' he thought.

Then he realized that his efforts to see over the fence had paid off in a surprising way. He had grown.

"Oh dear! Now I'm in trouble" he thought as he wandered home.

But he wasn't. In fact his family had been watching him absent-mindedly nibbling on juicy young green leaves high up in the trees.

Those leaves looked so good, they wanted some too but couldn't reach up that high. So they all started straining and stretching to become as tall as Raffy

... the first Giraffe!

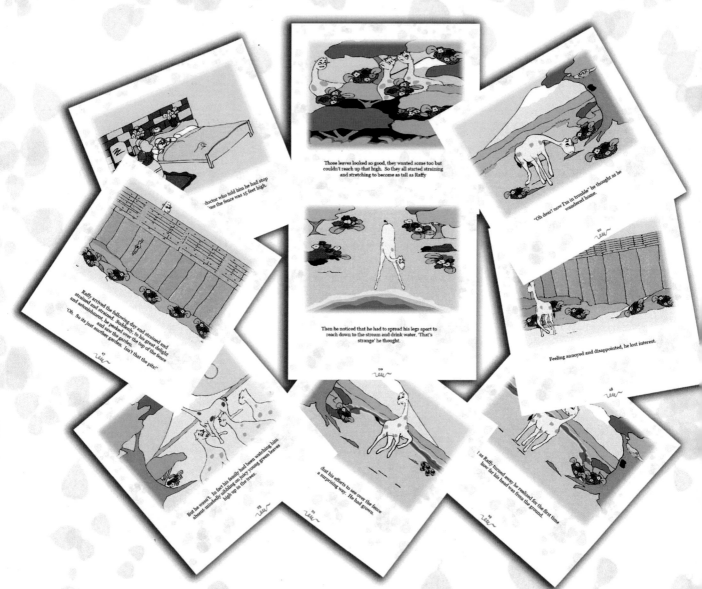

Visit www.creativestories.us and download your free animated, audio version of Raffy! See your beloved story come to life and grow together with Raffy in Karanga!

www.creativestories.us

where adventure begins...